CHINESE ZODIAC SIGNS

CHINESE ZODIAC SIGNS

YEAR OF THE RABBIT

1903 · 1915 · 1927
1939 · 1951 · 1963
1975 · 1987 · 1999

ARROW

Arrow Books Limited
17-21 Conway Street, London W1P 6JD
An imprint of the Hutchinson Publishing Group
London Melbourne Sydney Auckland
Johannesburg and agencies throughout the world
First published by M.A. Editions 1982
Arrow edition 1984
© M.A. Editions 1982

Produced by Aurum Press, 33 Museum Street, London WC1
Original text in French by Catherine Aubier
Translated by Eileen Finletter and Ian Murray
Designed by Julie Francis
Phototypeset in Optima
by York House Typographic, Hanwell, London
Made and printed in Great Britain
by Anchor Brendon Limited, Tiptree, Essex

ISBN 0 09 933450 X

CONTENTS

In the same series

THE RAT
1900-1912-1924-1936-1948
1960-1972-1984-1996

THE OX
1901-1913-1925-1937-1949
1961-1973-1985-1997

THE TIGER
1902-1914-1926-1938-1950
1962-1974-1986-1998

THE RABBIT
1903-1915-1927-1939-1951
1963-1975-1987-1999

THE DRAGON
1904-1916-1928-1940-1952
1964-1976-1988-2000

THE SNAKE
1905-1917-1929-1941-1953
1965-1977-1989-2001

THE HORSE
1906-1918-1930-1942-1954
1966-1978-1990-2002

THE GOAT
1907-1919-1931-1943-1955
1967-1979-1991-2003

THE MONKEY
1908-1920-1932-1944-1956
1968-1980-1992-2004

THE ROOSTER
1909-1921-1933-1945-1957
1969-1981-1993-2005

THE DOG
1910-1922-1934-1946-1958
1970-1982-1994-2006

THE PIG
1911-1923-1935-1947-1959
1971-1983-1995-2007

HOW TO USE THIS BOOK

Each section of this book gives a detailed description of the character, personality and partnership possibilities of the Rabbit. The characteristics of this sign are described in conjunction with the important ascendant sign.

There is also a synthesis of the Chinese zodiac and the more familiar Western zodiac. Together these give new meaning and depth to the description and prediction of an individual's personality, the main tendencies of his character, his behaviour and the broad outline of his destiny.

The book concludes with the fascinating astrological game, the I Ching.

The arrangement of the book is as follows:
A short introduction to the background and philosophy of the Chinese zodiac (page 8).
A description of the characteristics of your specific Chinese sign, determined by the *year of your birth* — in this case the Rabbit (page 19).
The best (and worst) partners for that Sign, determined by *the hour of your birth* (page 39).
The combination and interaction of your sign with the Ascendant Element: Earth, Water, Fire, Wood, Metal (page 48).
The comparison and combination of the two zodiacs — Chinese and Western (for example, the Sagittarian Rabbit, the Virgo Rabbit) — highlight many subtleties which enable you to clarify your psychological portrait (page 66).
The astrological game of the I Ching, which adapts the ancient Taoist 'Book of Mutations' to each Chinese sign. This simple game offers the reader the opportunity to obtain wise and appropriate answers to abstract as well as everyday questions (page 75).

THE MYSTERIES OF CHINESE ASTROLOGY

中國星相學之神秘

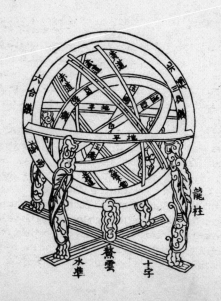

The legend of Buddha

One Chinese New Year more than five centuries before Christ, Buddha invited all the animals in creation to come to him, promising them recompense appropriate to his all-powerful and miraculous kindness and generosity. However, dimmed by their preoccupations of the moment (is it not said in the West that the characteristic of the animal is merely to eat, sleep, couple and fear?), almost all of them ignored the call of the Divine Sage. Yet twelve of the animals did go to him. They were, in order of their arrival, the Rat, Ox, Tiger, Rabbit, Dragon, Snake, Horse, Goat, Monkey, Rooster, Dog and Pig (other traditions replace the Rabbit with the Cat and the Pig with the Wild Boar).

To thank them Buddha offered each a year which would be dedicated to him alone through the ages. This year would carry the animal's name, and express his symbolic character and his specific psychological traits, marking the personality and behaviour of people born during that year.

Thus a cycle of twelve years was established, fitting exactly the sequence and rhythm of this improbable bestiary (one can imagine the dizzying amount of work which would have faced the astrologer if all of the animals had answered Buddha's invitation!).

Such is the legend.

The lunar cycle

Actually, Chinese astrology precedes the development of Far Eastern Buddhism, which began only in the 5th century of the Christian era, or about one thousand years after Buddha's appearance on earth. However, astrologers were already practising their art in China ten centuries before Christ; but the very origins of this astrology are as controversial as they are immemorial.

One point cannot be disputed: contrary to the West, which developed a solar astrology based on the apparent displacements of the daily star as its position in the Western zodiac changed from month to month, the Far East constructed a lunar astrology based on the annual cycle of lunar movements. This is why the Asian New Year — the Tet celebration among the Vietnamese — never falls exactly on the same date (page 93).

While the phases of the moon are equally important for a Western astrologer, their context is inscribed differently, with the result that their play of correspondence — and so their meanings and implications — are not comparable to those of Eastern astrology.

Without entering too deeply into scientific considerations which would lead us away from the purposes of this book, let us simply remind ourselves of the obvious and multiple influences of the moon, for example the movement of the tides, as well as more subtle levels, such as the female cycles and the obscure depths of the psyche. The term 'lunatic' has a precise and, indeed, clinical meaning. Recent statistical studies, for example, have made it possible to establish a strange and significant increase in acts of violence and criminality on nights when there is a full moon. Also, rigorous tests have established the direct impact of the moon on the chemical composition of certain bodies whose molecular structure can be modified depending on whether or not they have been exposed to lunar light.

Nuances of Chinese astrology

So, here we are with our twelve animals, the *Emblems* of Chinese astrology. Does this mean that all persons born in the same year as, say, the Rat or the Horse, will be subject to the same formulae of character and destiny? No more so than that those born under the sign of Aries or Libra are all confined to the same zodiacal script.

In Western astrology, the position of the planets, the calculation of the Ascendant and the Golden Mean of the Sky and its Mansions, allows the astrologer to refine and individualize a given theme considerably. In the same way, in Chinese astrology one obtains some surprisingly detailed and complex results. This is achieved by integrating with the intitial data factors such as the *Companion in Life* (determined by the hour of birth, but not to be confused with the Western Ascendant), and the predominant *Element*, which refers to the five Elements: Earth, Water, Fire, Wood and Metal.

This triple point of view — the *Emblematic Animal*, the *Companion in Life* and the *Element* — provide the reader with a greater diversity of references and a totality of perspectives both more rich and more precise than those found in Western astrology. To this we have added a detailed interpretation of the relationship between the Chinese and Western signs. The two astrologies are by nature distinct but never contradictory, and therefore complementary aspects and fusion can only result in a more profound understanding of the psychological types emanating from them. However, it is important to stress that although the concept of analogy holds an important place in Chinese astrology, it bears neither the same sense nor the same overall significance as in Western astrology.

Each Chinese sign is a universe in itself, a small cosmos

with its own laws and domains, completely independent of all other signs. Each of these living creatures is given specific powers and functions, becoming an emblematic animal endowed with a particular dimension peculiar unto itself. It creates its own jungle or cavern, and defines by its rhythm its own cadences and breathing. In this way it secretes its own chemistry — or, rather, its own alchemy. It is a supple, mobile, fluctuating image, governed by its own internal metamorphoses and contradictions.

Once we understand this, we will see that it is fatal to impose a fixed framework or clearly circumscribed area of mental categories and psychological equations in order to protect or reassure an anguished ego seeking a comforting or flattering projection of its own desires and fears.

Our alignment to a Chinese sign cannot be defined by exclusive formulae or linear classifications. The Chinese symbol unfolds slowly, a gift of the Gods, of Time and of Mystery; a delectable or poisoned gift which an Oriental person accepts with humility because he knows that its flavour may be born of the poison, as its poison may be born of the flavour.

Sometimes, in the course of a lifetime, it is circumstances more than a character trait which seem to determine and crystallize the principal tendencies of a sign. In such cases a thread of major or minor events will tend to form a symphonic background to the style of, say, a Dragon or a Rat.

To Have and To Be

Through the centuries Chinese astrology has permeated and inspired the mental attitudes and behaviour of hundreds of millions of people in the Far East, to an extent that is difficult for us to accept or even appreciate.

To understand better the spirit in which these people rely on the art of contemplation in handling the problems of daily life, a cardinal point must be emphasized — one which probably constituted the essential and fundamental difference between Eastern and Western civilizations, and poses a virtually impassable dividing line between them.

In our Western 'consumer society' — irrespective of the admiring or negative feelings we may associate with this expression — the fundamental question, from birth to death and at all levels of activity, is: *'What can I have?'*. We are continuously asking what we might possess or enjoy; what material goods, fortune, luck, honours or power might be had; whether we will achieve success in love, prestige, a good job, family, health, home, friends or, on another level, culture and knowledge. It is always a question of, 'What can I obtain, preserve, enlarge?' which underlies the totality of our motivations.

Think of the *models* that are held up to us: the successful politicians, business tycoons, film and stage stars, celebrated artists or scientist, sports champions, heroes of crime novels or comic strips. Idols of all kinds incarnate the triumph and glory of 'to have'. All will say, 'I have the most power, the most money, the most diplomas and abilities', or even, 'Mine is the greatest love affair'. Or, why not 'Mine is the most terrible drama, the most frightful illness'? Esteem is won exclusively from what one *has*.

Still more obvious is advertising, which is omnipresent today, and proclaims that one must absolutely *have* such and such a product in order *to be*: dynamic, seductive, happy, at ease with oneself or wholly fulfilled.

For Orientals, the decisive question is not *'What can I have?'* but *'Whom can I be?'* The model aspired to is not the great leader, the hero or the champion, but the poor, naked Sage who has attained total freedom and perfect peace within himself. Princes and great businessmen bow low before him, for he is the image of the highest self-realization possible to man. In this perspective, the Sage renounces nothing; on the contrary, since he has attained the supreme reality, he is immeasurably richer than the most powerful ruler.

It is we who, due to our fragmented and illusory

attachments, our infantile whims and our incessant conflicts, continually forgo the most marvellous felicity of all — God.

'*Who am I?*' Whatever approaches and methods, schools, sects or forms of asceticism are followed, this question, in appearance so simple and banal, lies at the base of and is the key to all Oriental culture. Through it lies the way to true liberation, by way of those roads to genuine understanding and knowledge known as Yoga, Vedanta, Tantra, Tao and Zen — to cite only the best known.

All this may cause the Chinese approach to astrology to seem disconcerting to us. The Oriental does not think '*I have* such and such predispositions, aptitudes or weaknesses inherent in my horoscope', but rather, 'How can I *be* a Rat (or a Goat or a Dog) in all the circumstances of my life?'

The Oriental's goal is not 'to have' in the same way in which we in the West say 'I possess such and such a quality or defect'. For him, it is instead a question of directions, implying a subtle and rhythmic progression; a sort of poetic dance of destiny, with each animal possessing its own steps and pirouettes — an entire choreography of its own.

These subtleties must be perceived clearly by those who wish to evolve without losing their way or turning round in circles in this immense domain of shimmering and shifting aspects of understanding.

The astrological I Ching

In the last section of this book, we present a game inspired by the oracles of the I Ching and adapted to each sign.

In his book *Zen Buddhism*, Alan Watts wrote: 'The I Ching is a work of divination containing oracles based on 64 abstract figures, each composed of six traits. These traits are of two sorts: divided or negative and undivided or positive. A modern psychologist would recognize an analogy with the Rorschach test, whose aim is to establish the mental portrait of an individual according to the spontaneous images suggested to him by an inkspot or an over-elaborate design. A subject whose images are inspired by the inkspot should be able to use his subsequent perceptions to deduce the necessary practical information to guide his future behaviour. Considered in this way, the divinatory art of the I Ching cannot be attacked as a vulgar superstition.'

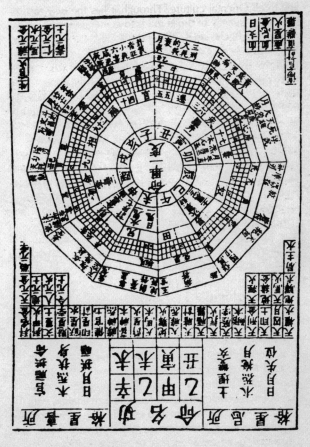

The relationship between the Signs and the Lunar Mansions

The practitioner of the I Ching commands an entire critical survey of the methods available when important decisions have to be made. We, on the other hand, are convinced that our decisions are rational because we depend upon a cluster of valid data affecting a problem; not for us to leave it to a mere game of heads or tails. The practitioner, however, might question whether we know what information is truly valid, given the fact that our plans are being constantly upset by events which are wholly unpredictable. Indeed, if we were rigorously rational in our choices of the data upon which our behaviour depended, so much time would be required that the moment for action would pass before we could assemble the data. Although we may set out initially to seek this information in a scientific manner, we are rapidly forced to act on another basis — capricious intuition, the impossibility of thinking further because we are too exhausted, or simply that time is too short and a choice must be made. In other words, our most important decisions are based largely on impressions, on our capacity to 'feel' a situation.

Every practitioner of the I Ching knows this. He is aware that his method is not an exact science but a useful and effective approach, if he is endowed with sufficient powers of intuition or, as he would say, 'in the Tao'.

THE YIN AND THE YANG

The *Yin* and the *Yang* are the symbols of two opposing and complementary principles whose indissoluble play and constant metamorphosis represent the roots, indeed the very tissues of the universe in action. They represent the eternal opposites — Positive-Negative, Yes-No, White-Black, Day-Night, Full-Empty, Active-Passive, Masculine-Feminine, and so on. Each contains within itself the germ of the other. That is why the man (Yang) bears within himself a feminine component (Yin), and the woman (Yin) a masculine one (Yang).

The Yin-Yang coupling is both indissoluble and changeable, each of the two terms being also its opposite and complementary term. This is expressed by the traditional figure:

At the moment when the Yang (white, active) is at its apogee — the bulging, enlarged part — the Yin (black, passive) imperceptibly takes its place — the tapering part — and vice versa.

The Yin and the Yang have no 'moral' character, neither is superior nor inferior to the other. Their antithesis is as necessary and as little in conflict as that of the left hand and the right hand striking together to applaud.

THE YIN AND THE YANG TYPES

The Rat, Ox, Rabbit, Monkey, Dog and Pig are **Yin**.
The Tiger, Horse, Dragon, Snake, Goat and Rooster are
Yang.

The Yin man

Appearance: The Yin man is often corpulent, of medium
height and muscularly well developed. He is physically
resilient to a marked degree and his health is sound. He
often has a round face and does not smile much.

Psychology: The Yin man is above all self-preoccupied and
inclined to consider himself the centre of the universe.
Though his behaviour appears calm, his moods are unstable
and susceptible to his immediate environment. He has great
confidence in himself, yet fears failure. Sociable, hospitable,
he is optimistic vis-à-vis himself and others. His life is active;
he is pragmatic and efficient.

The Yang man

Appearance: He is of average weight, often tall and slender,
even willowy. His face is smiling and he prefers strong
colours. Of delicate health, he should be advised to prevent
rather than wait to cure illness.

Psychology: The Yang man is an individualist and attracted
to introspective meditation. He is intelligent, independent
and at times solitary. He prefers his own company and
communing with nature to living with the crowd. Contrary
to the Yin man, he seeks his equilibrium within himself
instead of finding it amongst others.

THE DOMAINS
OF
THE RABBIT

十二生肖

THE RABBIT AND ITS SYMBOLISM

The Rabbit is of the Yin tendency; he keeps to the West and belongs to the full moon of mid-autumn.

This animal seems above all to exude a mysterious and elusive essence. It is often our own images which are reflected in our diverse representations of this familiar beast, rather than a true understanding of its nature. Solitary, unusual and enigmatic, the Rabbit is the incarnation of the unsolved mysteries of the world. Subtle and omnipresent, he is the child of dreams and of the night. This smooth, disquieting creature also crystallizes hate and violence, calling forth superstitions. In the Middle Ages, for example, it was a bad omen for a traveller to see a rabbit before setting out on his journey. Yet he also has a history of benevolence and good luck. In pagan times he was worshipped as a sacred animal associated with fertility and the rites of spring. The tradition of a rabbit's paw bringing good luck originates from the eighteenth-century belief that the right paw of a rabbit carried in the left-hand pocket would keep away rheumatism. And, on a more fanciful note, who can forget the wondrous White Rabbit in 'Alice in Wonderland'?

In China the rabbit is common to the Yangtze valley and is the symbol of longevity. For thousands of years he has been associated with the moon, tradition stating that he comes from its vital essence and is therefore strongly influenced by lunar energies. A Buddhist legend relates how a rabbit once offered itself as a willing sacrifice, lying down on a pile of dry grass beneath a full moon; as a reward its soul was delivered to the keeping of the moon.

The Rabbit is said to live one thousand years, turning completely white when it reaches the age of five hundred; a red hare is a symbol of luck and appears when virtuous rulers govern. A very old Taoist tale says that he is the servant of a genie and helps mix the elixir of life.

This little god with a thousand faces should not be tamed or imprisoned in a tiny universe, but should be followed along his path of dreams. His velvet, noiseless tread — is it not the echo of our own fantasies? And that coat of silk, that supple and agile body, are they not the reflection of our own dreams?

A few notes on the Rabbit

Principal qualities: Discreet, prudent, profoundly honest.
Principal defects: Easily offended, egotistic, sometimes pedantic.
Work: Serious and persevering. His motto could be 'It is no good hurrying, you must start punctually'.
Best role: Friend; no one can equal him.
Worst role: Reveller.
Money: Prudent where necessities are concerned; otherwise spendthrift.
Luck: To be born in summer. His destiny will be more serene and he will be less cold.
Cannot live without: A home port.
Adores: Intimate gatherings round a fire while the storm rages outside.
Hates: Being forced to make a decision or to take sides; extreme or conflicting situations, difficult choices.
Leisure activities: Enjoys everything, as long as he is not responsible for its organization or direction and does not have to take risks. Do not take him on an expedition without a first-aid kit.
Favourite places: Nocturnal and silent paths, preferably near his home; paths in the wilderness.
Colour: White.
Plant: Fig tree.
Flower: Queen Anne's Lace.
Professions: Philospher, diplomat, administrator, politician, priest. He can function in all roles except as a front-line fighter.

The four ages in the life of the Rabbit according to Chinese tradition

Rabbits' lives are likely to be peaceful in *childhood, youth, maturity* and *old age*, as long as they do not live in a time of war, revolution or other such conflict. Their destiny thus depends on external circumstances, the times in which they live and the persons they meet. Their *old age*, however, could be sad or solitary because of their inability or disinclination to make a definite choice.

THE PSYCHOLOGY OF THE RABBIT

Since time immemorial, Rabbits have caused a lot of ink to flow. They have been deified and had statues erected to them; they are at times the emblems of tranquil wisdom, at others the companions of demons. These animals, who cannot really be classified as being 'domestic', always provoke extreme reactions: it is their privilege to be either adored or detested. No one is truly indifferent to them.

In Chinese astrology this sign is one of the most difficult to describe accurately, for it is infinitely shaded and complex. It is as much of a feat to describe the Rabbit in simple and concrete terms as it is to learn acrobatics.

The first and most important ambivalence of the Rabbit is precisely this subtle alternation between dependence and savagery: a taste for comfort and a need for absolute liberty. One can spend a lifetime with a Rabbit in total hapiness, before becoming aware that he escapes all traps and adversaries. His attitude is unforseeable and sometimes ill-adapted to circumstances. When one expects him to be courageous, when there is an ordeal to be faced, he takes cover; when one thinks that he is going to flee, he bravely faces up to any snarling adversary.

This sensitive being, infinitely receptive to currents, climates and sensations, listens only to his intuition, remaining open to and at the disposal of vibrations rather than to analyses or reasoning. It is useless to discuss logic with a Rabbit, even when his profession or his form of intelligence requires that he deal with facts and figures. His real reactions will always lie behind his words, a subjective terrain in which his paws are firmly anchored.

Rabbits are adaptable and can appear to be tame. But if

they are not content with their life or with their environment, they will not show it but relegate their dissatisfaction to the recesses of their mysterious beings. If circumstances change, it may one day appear; but if circumstances remain as they are, it may never be expressed.

Like those animals appreciated by the 'fervent lovers and austere scholars' dear to the French poet Baudelaire, those born under this sign behave with discretion and moderation. They are living proofs of suppleness and diplomacy and take an infinite amount of trouble to avoid conflicts and to resolve disputes. Sensitive to harmony, they need a peaceful, temperate climate and a soft ambience in order to blossom. Morally demanding, naturally virtuous, prudent and reflective, they seek comfort, security and tranquillity.

Throughout their lives, Rabbits work to consolidate the structures which make up their psychological and material 'crutches'. Their universe is first and foremost the immediate and the visible. It is only when they have turned everything round in their minds, sniffed in all the corners and provided all the doors with security systems, that they dare go a bit further — but still with prudence and circumspection, carefully placing one paw after the other, watchful, on the alert and vigilant.

This apprehensive attitude derives from the fear nourished by every Rabbit of the disruptions which might unsettle his life. For this sign is neither combative nor aggressive. A Rabbit never derives pleasure from throwing himself head first into difficulties. In fact, he does all he can to avoid them and it is only when he finds himself cornered in an extreme or tense situation that he can be forced into a fight. Rabbits only become dangerous when they are at bay, when baring their teeth is the only resource left to them. Otherwise, they flee from combat and avoid arguments, which they detest.

Their defects include a tendency to hesitate and to be faint-hearted. They do not like to move forward without knowing exactly what lies ahead; they are not made for suspense. Their usual policy is to protect their rear, while

23

examining future possibilities; often, they simply remain in place and miss their opportunities.

Rabbits' deep attachment to security frequently makes them seem indifferent, which they are not, and egotists, which they are. Their moral well-being is essential to them and, although they love to do someone a god turn, they will never do so to the extent of questioning their principles. It may be difficult to believe they are so morally virtuous, but they sincerely believe in the pretexts they put forth.

Rabbits are agreeable to live with, for they are peaceful, sociable and easy-going; they are rarely irritable, remain calm and keep their heads. They are attentive and faithful friends, extremely hospitable, warm, refined and full of delicacy, accepting it as their duty to be understanding and tolerant. Abiding by honourable principles and respectful of traditions, they are rather easily shocked and offended. Just as they are discreet in public, so they love to shine and feel appreciated within their own circle. They express themselves with ease and elegance on many subjects, and their subtlety and facility for assimilation helps them to appear well informed about everything. Not only do they take pride in cultivating their minds, they like others to profit from what they have learned. Rabbits detest being left out of a discussion.

Perfectly at ease in daily life, whose responsibilities they assume easily enough, Rabbits are disturbed by unforeseen situations. Generally, a Rabbit can master any difficulty provided he has also mastered a knowledge of its various aspects and can pull the strings; otherwise he will be nervous, will panic and be inefficient. Most Rabbits are like this. Their success and happiness are dependent on a great variety of circumstances, including external forces at work in the world at large. Peaceful animals, Rabbits are not made for revolutions.

THE RABBIT AS A CHILD

The child born during a year of the Rabbit is usually a delight to bring up. On the whole obedient and disciplined, he rarely questions his parents' advice. He is smiling and approachable, happy to do a good turn, does his homework carefully and spontaneously takes part in school games. But in these and other sports he rarely takes risks, for he is really rather timorous. His parents will have no need to worry about the creases in his trousers or the need to keep bottles of iodine to hand for his wounds; he will prefer the awards of being 'first in the class' to those of the playing fields.

In some cases the young Rabbit is a little lacking in imagination, which may protect him from making stupid errors but will also prevent him from making discoveries on his own. He needs to be stimulated by his parents, which is not a difficult tast for he is adaptable and learns rapidly. His passivity stems from a distaste for personal involvement, and it is only this which restrains his young curiosity. To be truly comfortable and at ease the Rabbit child needs a corner to himself, ideally his own room. If this is not possible, try to arrange a private corner for him, even if it is only protected by a screen, and allow him to arrange this intimate space according to his fancy. He must learn to construct his own personal environment.

If the Rabbit child cries at night, gripped by irrational terrors, reassure him by persuading him that his fears are irrational. But do not pamper him; he needs to become accustomed to the unforeseen and learn to accept risks if he is to confront difficulties later in life. If he is pampered too much, this lunar acrobat and tightrope walker will grow up to be a greedy glutton, plump and wheezing.

Intelligent and diligent, the Rabbit child is likely to do well at school, which will make him slightly vain. One should watch over his choice of subjects for, lacking critical sense in such matters, he is in danger of being too persistent and succeeding in a profession which does not really interest him. He is sensitive to conditioning, heredity, the value of the example and he likes to give pleasure. Remember that he is a Rabbit — and do not try to teach him to fly.

LOVE LIFE

All Rabbits love to be loved; and, because they are far form being fools, it does not take them long to understand that the best way to get love is to give it — before it is given. Consequently they are charming with those from whom they wish to receive affection, as well as with those whom they esteem. They are attentive, affectionate, tender, never forget a birthday and are sensitive to the needs of those around them.

In a climate of shared love, Rabbits blossom and diffuse an aura of happiness. But they need active and constant warmth or all this will fade away. They must feel secure and know that they are loved — that is their oxygen.

Rabbits are faithful and tender by nature and because of their respect for convention. They breathe uneasily during storms of passion and constantly attempt to simplify complex situations in order to feel secure again. If there is too much conflict around them or a situation becomes too tense, they will leave; and if that proves impossible, they will become ill.

Certain Rabbits flit about incessantly and an uninformed observer may think them to be unfaithful, superficial and egotistical. In fact, their inconstant behaviour and fickle seductions express their deep need for a safe home port. As long as their experiences and encounters with others do not seem worthy of their total involvement, they continue to frolic, their ears pricked up. Then one day they meet the provider of the nest they have always dreamt of, and you can be sure that they will then do everything possible not to lose it.

Rabbits detest partings and will hope against all reason that life will untangle the threads of the relationship without wounds or rancour and restore them to their place in the sun.

FAMILY LIFE

Although Rabbits value marriage, intimacy and close

friendships, they sometimes feel ill at ease as parents. It is not that they neglect or scorn their children; in fact, they are indulgent to the point of spoiling them. They will do anything to rear successfully the little marvels they have brought into the world — including a certain toughness, the attitude of a mother rabbit defending its young, even if the emotional relationship is difficult.

While adoring their little ones, Rabbits are easily put out by the great and small upheavals which children inflict on their well-regulated lives. When their children are infants, subject to the hourly feedings and immobilized in a crib, our Rabbits will handle the situation brilliantly. But as soon as the charming baby begins to crawl everywhere, smear the walls and knock over flower vases, things will start to go wrong. Rabbit parents, not being authoritarian by nature, waver between uncontrollable laughter and anger. Many of them, unable to cope, hide behind indifference; the most energetic try to give their offspring a sense of discipline which, with some signs, is indeed a risk.

Everything will go well with Ox, Dog, Snake, Goat, Pig or Rabbit children. Monkey and Rat children will confuse their parents, who will wonder constantly what new catastrophe their child is going to come up with. The independent nature of the Dragon, Tiger and Horse will upset the tranquillity of a father or mother Rabbit considerably.

However this may be, Rabbits, without being slaves to their families — they also attach great importance to their social lives — go to some lengths to preserve harmony. They also know how to find peace and happiness in their daily life: female Rabbits adore housekeeping and receiving guests. But once the word 'divorce' is mentioned, our peace-loving friends are transformed into furious spitting and anxious tigers. For Rabbits, the destruction of harmony is unbearable.

PROFESSIONAL LIFE

Because of his prudence, tact and diplomacy, the Rabbit is

well suited to any profession that involves harmonious relations with others. In short, he can do anything and sustain any role — except, perhaps, that of Robinson Crusoe.

So, you may ask, why do we not see more Rabbits at the top of their professions? There are several reasons. First of all, Rabbits are modest and not given to pretension. Often capable of doing better than others — thanks to their meticulousness, professional conscience and honesty — they forget to push themselves forwards, leaving the brilliant Dragons or the swashbuckling Roosters to reap the laurels that they themselves merit.

In general, Rabbits are limited in their ambitions: to succeed in their personal, emotional and family lives matters more to them than receiving an award. They refuse a life of compromise which such achievements depend on, dislike complicated plans and hate to get their hands dirty. At most they will ask their subordinates to wash the dirty linen. If they must retaliate, they will command the firing squad from a distance, considering such extreme measures as a 'necessary evil', preferring to set an example through gentleness. Rabbits know instinctively how to avoid conflict.

The more stable professions suit Rabbits best; they like to be recognized and appreciated and feel uneasy in vague situations. They are excellent executors, are organized, precise and like work well done, but are often brought up short if they must innovate, create or start again from the beginning. They adapt very well to changes but do not provoke them. They bloom better in an administrative position — whether it be in the world of finance or research — than in a liberal profession. Rabbits also do not enjoy wars of words, debates or heated arguments. While they prefer to work in a group rather than alone, they tend to leave discussion to others. They try to avoid exposing themselves to criticism, which can upset them considerably and even take away all their self-confidence.

Rabbits are remarkably gifted for the study of history, thanks to their excellent memory, which is quite exceptional; but although this is useful on a professional level, it can become a handicap emotionally, for there are times when it is best to know how to forget.

MATERIAL LIFE

Due to their need for security, Rabbits generally choose the winning side. If unsure they will adopt a neutral position so that their sudden about-faces are not too visible. From idealism they will sometimes uphold the weak side, but at the least sign of real risk they will soon rally to the strong. However, they should not be accused of selfishness or cowardice, because they are the first to suffer from their ambivalence. Sincerely compassionate and generous, they nevertheless lack the strength to do their utmost for a cause — unless, of course, their personal life or the well-being of their family is threatened and therefore dependent on the firmness of their stand.

Rabbits are not really selfish and not at all stingy; they simply plan exactly how much is needed for them to live protected from the unforeseen and, as a result, lack for nothing. It is easier for them to do this if they choose a stable profession within an administrative context, which they usually do.

Once their bank account is well-filled, they will establish deposit accounts for their family, prudence being the mother of security. But this is where their financial know-how completely crumbles: assuming, rightly or not, that they have paid tribute to the prudence which guides them, they easily become spendthrift and unwise, squandering any surplus funds on clothes, decorative objects, rich furnishings, sumptuous parties, travel and so on. It is, perhaps, for this reason that Rabbits frequently remain in a moderate financial position: avarice and hoarding are as foreign to them as the Tiger's love of taking financial risks. Between the two extremes, they eventually find a happy medium.

Intuitive rather than analytical, the Rabbit will sense what is going on around him; his spontaneous judgement is more accurate than his reasoning, which is often obscured by subjective factors.

ENVIRONMENT

Being excessively sensitive to atmosphere, Rabbits attach great importance to their daily lives. They love all that is beautiful and comfortable and, whatever their financial situation, they try to give their homes a touch of refinement, a special perfume. While not necessarily impeccable in their taste, they are orderly, meticulous and zealous house-keepers, known to become ill at the sight of a grease spot on a new rug. Rabbits love to entertain and go to a lot of trouble to treat their guests as royally as possible. They will find out in advance the special tastes of each guest, and will think nothing of preparing a special dish for the one who is slimming. Their guests will be greeted by a blazing fire and vases of freshly cut flowers — part of a Rabbit's natural hospitality.

Even in their offices or in a place they are only visiting, Rabbits know how to create a warm and cosy atmosphere which is special to them. With them, everyone feels at home. Their tastes in furnishing and decoration are rather classical, if not conservative. They adore pretty objects, old lace, candlesticks and romantic paintings. From time to time one finds a horror hanging on their wall, but it is usually a gift from a friend whom they do not want to upset; its sentimental value is worth more to them than its aesthetic or financial value.

Moving house is really heart-rending for them. They can remain for years in a crumbling flat without being able to decide to change. If you have a Rabbit child or friend, open a deposit account for him and oblige him to move.

A guide to relations with a Rabbit

Methods of seduction: For both sexes it begins with a long period of reflection: 'Is it a good match? Is his sincerity total? Can I count on his fidelity?' Finally, at the very moment that you are getting ready to search for more hospitable pastures, he — or she — will literally leap on you saying that he cannot possibly resist you.

If he loves you: It is up to you to take the initiative. You are so intelligent! He will let you speak first and you will be the first to enter his house. If the ceiling falls on you, he will care for you tenderly. But do not complain too loudly because he detests crying and blood.

He expects of you: That you insist that he accompany you to social events, but that you leave his mind free.

To keep you: He will be exceptionally patient and understanding.

If he is unfaithful: Him? never! It is all in your imagination. Anyway, it is his body, not his soul, which is all yours, and he will continue to plead innocent all the way to the scaffold.

If you are unfaithful: He will not make a scene because he hates them. But he will question you remorselessly and will even look in your pockets, feeling guilty all the while.

In case of a break between you: It will not be permanent unless you become truly odious. But do not count on him to take the initiative.

If you wish to give him a gift: You have the choice between a huge patchwork quilt, a soft cushion — or a James-Bond type bodyguard.

If you want to seduce him: Tell him that you represent a company handling bullet-proof doors and wish to show him the latest model. Be well supplied with cushions, have a fire lit and soft music playing.

If you want to get rid of him: Suggest that he join a terrorist group.

THE RABBIT
AND OTHER CHINESE SIGNS

Rabbit/Rat

Delighting in tranquillity and harmony, persons born during the year of the Rabbit hate extreme situations and are ill-equipped to deal with strain or stress.

The Rat, not realizing that his native disquiet creates a common ground with these graceful animals, will immediately label the Rabbit's prudence as pusillanimity. The latter will bristle at the Rat's tart criticism.

There is an undeniable, deep-rooted antipathy between the Rat and the Rabbit; if a Rat loves a Rabbit, he will not understand that the latter is at one and the same time adaptable, unstable and yet clings to security. And the Rat will have nothing to do with tranquillity and harmony; he prefers to live balanced on a tightrope, ever liable to have his fingers burnt. It is, of course, well known that the maxim 'once bitten, twice shy' applies to the Rabbit. Therefore, although the two have to make a strong effort to live together on an emotional level, as brother and sister or as friends, their differences can provide the opportunity for a profitable experience.

Rabbit/Ox

This combination is ideal! The Rabbit needs security, calmness and harmony, and the calm and stable Ox offers such a sanctuary. Sometimes the Rabbit is unfaithful — more to prove to himself his seductive powers than through a taste for infidelity — but above all, he values his home life. The Ox, who is not in the habit of going through his spouse's pockets, will prefer to remain as unsuspicious as he is faithful. Both of them fear financial setbacks, disagreeable and unforeseen events and personal confrontations. They always strive to secure their home from any possible hazard.

The Ox, being more independent and better armed to confront difficulties than the Rabbit, is better suited as the active element in this partnership. If his lack of diplomacy causes problems, the more supple and opportunistic Rabbit will give him useful advice.

There is only one obstacle: the Ox likes clear and plain answers, while the Rabbit is hesitant, uncertain, a little unsure and needs to work around a problem to find the ideal solution. By then the Ox will have made his own decision.

This union, while emotionally rich, is ill adapted for business unless there is a third party — a Tiger, for example — to appreciate, and therefore diminish, the risks involved.

Rabbit/Tiger

Both in their different ways seek to secure their prey. Each is attached to a certain form of comfort and they share the need for an impression of freedom. Rabbits and Tigers alike will settle by the fireside and then depart, if the mood takes them, to spend the night under the stars. Any attempt to constrain these two is inadvisable.

The Rabbit, however, is more dependent on a life of security, is much more prudent and is likely to shudder with horror at the Tiger's dare-devilry.

If the Rabbit is the less active of the two, their liaison will go very well. The Rabbit will take care of daily comforts and will discreetly restrain his companion's outbursts of audacity. If the contrary, life will be difficult. The undomesticated Tiger with nothing much to do will be furious whenever he sees his Rabbit spouse check the gas meters or the locks on the doors. He could easily lope out of his own house and return to burgle it.

When they disagree, the Rabbit will have a lighter touch than the Tiger; more agile, he will always have the last word, leaving the Tiger spinning round in circles.

Rabbit/Rabbit

One cannot see why two Rabbits should not succeed in getting along together. They take such trouble to preserve harmony that the least dispute would be nipped in the bud; the least sly spirit of discord would be whisked away by an angel of light as if by the wave of a magic wand to restore perfect harmony.

What our Rabbits risk is a lack of dynamism; they may go to sleep for too long. But if one is ambitious and the other sedentary, there is no doubt that their life will become a model for family magazines. One can well imagine them receiving awards for conjugal merit.

If the world is ablaze and in turmoil, you can be sure of finding a refuge with them — unless they have transformed their house into an impenetrable nuclear shelter.

Rabbit/Dragon

This relationship will be possible if it is the Dragon who wears the trousers — literally and figuratively. To live for any length of time with his sensational partner — who is not content merely to shine, but needs to collect several awards of distinction that he guards in a small engraved box — a

Rabbit needs to be philosophic and self-sacrificing, qualities he definitely lacks.

Rabbits are patient and peace-loving, but they do not like their paws to be stepped on, whereas Dragons are born paw-crushers. For a while the Rabbit will stoically endure this hurricane which several times a day devastates his chest of drawers, changes objects around and creates draughts (slamming doors are extremely perturbing to the well-bred Rabbit). So, one day, he will confront the Dragon — and it will not be the Dragon who has the last word, for Rabbits only appear to be weak. On the other hand, if the Dragon works away from home and the Rabbit keeps house, each will be free to organize his environment as he wishes, and everything will go well.

Rabbit/Horse
This combination is possible if the Rabbit is very much in love, for love makes him pliable. He is a sentimental and slightly romantic person, and the Horse's enthusiasm, warmth and passion will be irresistible to the Rabbit, who often hesitates to put himself forward; he will be admiring and breathless before the Horse's self-assurance. But when the Horse, in one of his spectacular changes of mood to which he is so often subject, collapses, saying that he is no good and that life is not worth living, the Rabbit will be able to comfort and coddle him.

Rabbit/Snake
They have in common a love of peace, security and aesthetic taste. They will tend to give preference to their home, environment and comfort and will appreciate beautiful objects and places. They would make a good pair of decorators. To have peace the Rabbit will have the wisdom to let the Snake think that he is the boss and master — at least on the emotional level. But the Rabbit's hesitations, and above all his virtuous side, will annoy the Snake whose sense of values is much more elastic.

However, whether it be love or friendship, this tie will be

profitable for both. With patience, the Rabbit will perhaps succeed in persuading the Snake to accept another's opinion; and the Snake, who does not fear danger and adapts to all situations, will teach the Rabbit to be more philosophic.

Rabbit/Goat

A very good alliance. Like the Rabbit, the Goat likes tranquillity, and he adapts to almost any kind of life which allows a minimum of liberty and offers him enough grass to graze on. The Rabbit is affectionate without being too possessive, and his love for the home brings an element of security to those in need of it.

The imagination and fantasy of the Goat will delight the Rabbit and help him escape the daily rut he has a tendency to fall into. The Rabbit's seriousness and his habit of perseverance promise well for the family finances. However, this couple will be vulnerable if an external crisis, a professional setback, an unforeseen loss of money or a domestic accident should occur, for the Rabbit and Goat find it difficult to depend on each other, and their relationship may be difficult to preserve. With each suffering from acute anxiety — the Rabbit for the future, the Goat for the present — they risk making mountains out of molehills and over-dramatizing everything.

Rabbit/Monkey

The intelligent and wily Monkey knows very well how to manage his affairs, but from time to time he enjoys finding understanding and rest with the indulgent and discreet Rabbit. The Rabbit knows all about wiliness, using it himself to get out of many a difficult situation. The Monkey's advice will enable the Rabbit to add several strings to his bow by making him more reasonable.

These two can attain a form of intimacy and complicity which is extremely personal and from which most people will feel excluded. Moreover, they will be so interested in each other that they will barely wish to raise a large family.

In business their understanding can be ticklish because the Rabbit, who is strongly attached to principles, will be scandalized by the occasional nearly illegal convolutions of the Monkey. He will criticize him, even though at bottom he envies him, and the Monkey will make fun of the Rabbit and disregard his virtuous indignation.

Rabbit/Rooster

Whether their relationship is based on friendship, love or professional ties, this duo often risks ending in a fist fight. In fact, no Rabbit has the patience needed to endure the swaggerings and boastings of the Rooster, who often exaggerates — most of the time without reason — just to amuse himself or to see how people react.

The usually patient and peaceful Rabbit will watch his tolerance evaporate quickly. The Rooster makes him literally boil, and our Rabbit cannot stop himself from wanting to snatch at some of the Rooster's feathers in order to diminish his vanity. The Rooster, who actually has no bad intentions, will see the Rabbit's attitude as one of malice — and he will not be entirely wrong.

If the Rabbit is the male, he will seek to confine Mrs Rooster to a role of submissive housekeeper, she, in turn will take advantage of his first absence to fly out the window. If the Rooster is the male, his Rabbit wife will criticize him ceaselessly, which he will not understand.

Rabbit/Dog

With luck, this can result in a happy and stable union. Although commonly regarded as hereditary enemies, these two animals — astrologically and psychologically speaking — have many points in common. Both seek security, both are profoundly honest, even virtuous, and both fiercely protect their property. They will understand, listen to and reassure each other.

But what is the small factor of luck that is needed? It lies in the absence of any great social and political event occurring during the course of their lives together. If such an event should occur, the Dog will heroically swallow his fear and join up as a nurse, missionary or even as cook, since he will do anything to feel useful. The Rabbit, who detests trouble, will ponder for years whether or not to follow him.

Rabbit/Pig

The award for merit and honesty goes to this couple. There is no doubt about it: they will appreciate each other for their true value, holding in esteem those qualities with which they are both bursting. When the Pig wants solitude, the Rabbit will lead his life quietly, perhaps using the time to repaint their flat. Together, these two will carefully avoid revolutions and earthquakes. The intuitive Rabbit will help his Pig spouse to not be taken in by all the tricksters who pass by and, without annoying him, will advise him and make him aware of his errors. There is only one danger: the Pig is sensual, even somewhat lascivious, whereas the Rabbit is slightly prudish, believing that even the most passionate liaisons should be veiled in platonic sentiments and not displayed publicly. The Pig will burst out laughing at this idea and offer the Rabbit a copy of the 'Kama-Sutra'. The Rabbit will not find this terribly amusing.

SOME RABBIT CELEBRITIES

Anne Boleyn, Bolivar, Bonnard, Carlyle, Fidel Castro, Chardin, Agatha Christie, Confucius, Courbet, Marie Curie, Einstein, Max Ernst, Garibaldi, Grieg, Keats, Paul Klee, Luther, Catherine de Medici, Henry Miller, Offenbach, Eva Peron, Edith Piaf, Pirandello, Prokofiev, Racine, Raphael, Rommel, Schiller, Walter Scott, Simenon, Stalin, Stendhal, Toscanini, Trotsky, Queen Victoria, Orson Welles.

YOUR COMPANION IN LIFE

生命伴侶

After the Chinese sign of your year of birth, here is the sign of your hour of birth

What is a Companion in Life, as understood in Chinese astrology? It is a sort of 'ascendant' sign corresponding to your hour of birth. This Companion is another animal belonging to the Chinese cycle of the twelve emblematic beasts, who falls into step with you and accompanies you, ever ready to help you brave the traps and ambushes along your route. A permanent and benevolent shadow, he can render the impossible possible.

He is your counterpart, but with his own character and tendencies and with a different psychology. Both guardian angel and devil's advocate, he will be a witness to your life and an actor in it.

Have you ever felt, deep inside yourself, the subtle presence of another 'myself' inhabiting you and with whom you live, at times in harmony, at others in conflict? Another self who sometimes criticizes you and at others encourages you? That is your Companion in Life.

There are times when he will appear to be an imposter or an intruder. Certainly, he often questions your habits and your moral or spiritual complacency. Accompanied by this companion, a shadow within, the route is less monotonous and the voyager multiplies his chances of arriving at his chosen destination. This, however, in itself matters little, for it is the journey and the manner in which it is conducted that are important. Indolence is the greatest danger: your Companion is capable of arousing you from a lassitude of spirit and, to that end, if necessary, robbing you of your certainties, trampling on your secret gardens and, finally, tearing away the great veil of illusion.

It sometimes happens that your Companion is of the same sign as your year of birth, a twin brother in a way — for example, a Rabbit/Rabbit. In this case, you must recognize that he will compel you to realize yourself fully and to live the double aspect — the Yin and the Yang — that your bear within yourself. In any case, you also bear within yourself the twelve animals. So, set out on the long route, ready for the great adventure: the beautiful voyage during which you will encounter the harmoniously entangled, the solemn and the grotesque, the ephemeral reality, the dream and the imagined.

Table of hours corresponding to the twelve emblematic animals

If you were **born** between		your **companion** is	
11 pm and	1 am		Rat
1 am and	3 am		Ox
3 am and	5 am		Tiger
5 am and	7 am		Rabbit
7 am and	9 am		Dragon
9 am and	11 am		Snake
11 am and	1 pm		Horse
1 pm and	3 pm		Goat
3 pm and	5 pm		Monkey
5 pm and	7 pm		Rooster
7 pm and	9 pm		Dog
9 pm and	11 pm		Pig

These figures correspond to the *solar hour* of your birth. If necessary, you should check the summer times (Daylight Savings Time) and make the appropriate adjustment (sometimes two hours before or after statutory time).

THE RABBIT AND ITS COMPANION IN LIFE

Rabbit/Rat

This is a curious mixture, to say the least. Are not these hereditary enemies 'condemned' to travel the same route? But do not be fooled, for this may be the best way to accomplish the voyage. An apprehensive Rat coupled with the eternally stalking Rabbit will not be easily deceived. Suspicious, both adaptable and aggressive, he will be ready to protect himself from predators and to go to any lengths to secure his comfort and vested interests. Also, the influence of the Rabbit will make the Rat less vulnerable to outbursts of passion. Calm and efficient, the Rat/Rabbit illustrates the aphorism 'Better to risk an intelligent friend than indulge a stupid one.'

Rabbit/Ox

A home-loving conqueror! The route will be difficult: the Ox/Rabbit will oscillate between anger and silence, and will hesitate between leaving entirely and retiring into contemplation. If at times the Rabbit element is a sort of ball-and-chain on the Ox, this will have its uses. Knowing in certain situations how to inspire prudence, calm anger and unknot nerves, the Rabbit can soften the stubbornness in which the Ox becomes entangled and stifled. Meanwhile, Ox will teach his Companion that real space and liberty cannot be measured by surface area alone, such as the size of the Rabbit's burrow. Which will win out — prudence or stubbornness? Take care, Ox/Rabbit, you are in danger of going round the world without leaving your room.

Rabbit/Tiger

Be careful of this animal; its appearance is deceptive. All gentleness on the outside — softly furry and velvety — he is mistakenly trusted. What makes the Tiger makes the Rabbit, and what makes the Rabbit makes the Tiger — all the better to eat you up. The Rabbit in the skin of a Tiger will find himself perfectly at ease; as for the Tiger, what could be easier than to give the illusion of being a harmless, large, striped tomcat. Essentially, game for the Tiger/Rabbit will involve sowing illusions and creating confusion among other animals: imagine Rudyard Kipling's Tiger meeting up with Bugs Bunny.

 Rabbit/Rabbit

He is a mysterious and enigmatic animal, who cultivates a pronounced taste for secrecy; nothing is simple or self-evident for him. Morbidly prudent (he will plan his route meticulously, foreseeing a host of eventual difficulties and how to avoid them), his journey will be transformed into a marathon. Do not hope to get the better of him while he is asleep: he sleeps with one eye open and the other on the look-out. The Rabbit/Rabbit will be a great seducer, refined and perceptive, but beneath his velvet paws, his claws are never completely drawn in. This lover of hiding places and comfortable nooks should overcome his fear of giving himself in a relationship; otherwise he may end up in a lonely corner.

Rabbit/Dragon

This companion will bring him self-confidence, and he will feel his wings growing, be they made of lace or scales. The Rabbit/Dragon will be audacious, equipped with a lively and shrewd intelligence. He will be a seductive prince endowed with a complex brain; a mysterious being gliding among fairy-like worlds and parallel universes. However, he should be wary of a type of aggressiveness revealed in an attitude of 'I know everything; I have seen everything'. He is the guardian of a secret or treasure and has the soul of a fantasist; a lunar vagabond with magical powers, in search of the marvellous.

 Rabbit/Snake

A strange creature, whose head is not easily distinguished from its tail. In love with anything strange, but not an adventurer, the Snake/Rabbit will daydream about travelling while curled up in a soft armchair. 'Inhabited' by a price of wanderings, he has a taste for suspense, mystery and the subterranean, discovering hiding places buried under a stone. He will not hesitate to take on the colour of a wall for the pleasure of deceiving, surprising and disconcerting you. Elusive, clever and shifty, he is as dangerous as he is seductive. If you meet up with a Snake/Rabbit, pinch yourself, because he is a professional spell-binder. He will seduce you somehow — with his charm or by blackmail.

Rabbit/Horse

Something of an unprincipled opportunist, he will be slightly mystifying. Irresistibly attracted by all that glitters, he will alternate between being impetuous and prudent. The Horse/Rabbit is a winner; he refuses to run for cover, even when security requires it. For him, a thrilling route is a necessity, and he obtains his goals. This war-horse will not allow others to step on his toes or obstruct him.

 Rabbit/Goat

He will be a sweet dreamer, living far from reality in a world of clouds. If he cannot find the comfort which is so dear to him, he will seek it in his dreams. He will love travel, always seeking something more marvellous. He has a supple nature and is intuitive and charming; nothing will seem to ruffle him, for he has the gift of assimilating the most trying situations into his creative universe. Both collar and leash will be rejected by the Goat/Rabbit for he is the type who is always on the loose, ever-ready for adventure.

Rabbit/Monkey

He will be an inventive, lively, rather airy animal. He will have a tendency to be calculating, and will leave nothing to chance. He prefers being a schemer, conjuror and scrounger to labourious and irksome work. The Monkey/Rabbit envisages life as a game which, for the fun of it, he himself strews with traps and mirages, the better to zigzag between them. To attain his ends, he throws scruples to the wind. He will not hesitate to cheat, but who is he deceiving? He does not know himself, unless one day the Sphinx asks him the question.

 Rabbit/Rooster

He will always keep his eyes peeled. He must always be entitled to the right to look, to control a situation and to feel he is the master of his destiny. He is not the kind to let himself be guided. He is a curious mixture in which the call of the dawn is coupled with the murmurs of the night. The voyage will be profitable if the prudence of the Rabbit is allied with the tenacity and loyalty of the Rooster. The Rabbit/Rooster is a generous, lively animal with a pure heart. His spur and his claw will be used defensively rather than offensively.

Rabbit/Dog

In this person the Dog element should be recognized as a guide and guardian, a faithful Companion into the invisible world which lies beyond the voyage of life. The egotistical Rabbit will discover that a precious ally lies within him. The Dog/Rabbit is circumspect, sometimes to the point of sickly distrust. While the sun may be shining on him, he will still be thinking only of the darkness to come. This animal is incapable of living in the present and has a tendency to become obsessed with past failures and future difficulties. He will weep for himself, his often imagined ills, and be depressed by the size of his task! In such moods he is incapable of looking at the simple spectacle of life going on around him, let alone enjoying it.

 Rabbit/Pig

A solitary animal who is slightly disquieting but perfectly organized. There exists an air of mystery about him; one never knows the real truth. Amassing great wealth, he lives in luxurious comfort but without neglecting the cultivation of his mind. Seductive, he is given to good and bad excesses, a distinction he prefers to ignore. If you corner him, he may either slip away or attack — unless he merely gives you a reply that leaves you breathless. This Rabbit/Pig is often master of a palace of mirages constructed on a base of others' gullibility.

THE RABBIT
AND THE FIVE
ELEMENTS

五行

YOUR ELEMENT

In Chinese astrology, each year is joined to an Element. There are five Elements: *Water, Fire, Wood, Metal, Earth.*

Each of the twelve emblematic animals is linked successively to each of the five Elements. For example, in the year 1900 the Rat was Earth, in 1912 he was Fire; in 1924 he was Metal, in 1936, Water and in 1948 he was Wood. Therefore, for the twelve years from 1900 he was linked to Earth, for the next twelve years to Fire, and, for every succeeding period of twelve years, to each of the other Elements, in succession.

In order to determine the Element corresponding to the year of your birth, use the table below:

> *Years whose digits end in:* 1 and 6 — Water
>
> 2 and 7 — Fire
>
> 3 and 8 — Wood
>
> 4 and 9 — Metal
>
> 5 and 0 — Earth

The same union of *Animal-Element* repeats every sixty years, for example, Rat-Earth appeared in 1720, 1780, 1840, 1900, 1960 and so on.

The five Elements are the primary forces affecting the universe. It is their particular association with each of the signs which provides the basis for every horoscope. Movement and fluctuation, Yin and Yang, these symbolic forces are in a perpetual state of action and interaction.

Wood gives birth to Fire, which gives birth to Earth, which gives birth to Metal, which gives birth to Water, which in turn gives birth to Wood.

RABBIT/WATER
(you were born in 1951)

The cold born of the northern sky descended to Earth and gave birth to Water. The Chinese consider Water more a synonym for coldness and ice than a symbol of fertility.

Characteristics of the Rabbit/Water

Water of winter nights, cold, rigour and severity; calm and deep Water to be feared and respected, still Water sheltering underwater demons asleep in its depths; foetid and muddy Water of the marshes, a refuge of crawling creatures.

Although not a fanatic about swimming, the Rabbit/Water wil feel at ease in this still water — unless it becomes a swamp, which could quickly absorb him, plunging him into a perilous situation while simultaneously reinforcing his tendency to inaction and a fear of becoming involved. Snug and warm, he can construct a cosy refuge in it and allow himself to be swallowed up; unless it is cold and clear and the Rabbit uses it to remedy his sluggishness.

Health of the Rabbit/Water

The Water organ is the kidney; its flavour is salty. Take care not to lie too long in fresh water: its tonic effect soon wears off and becomes merely soothing. Look after your spine and kidneys; do not remain inactive.

The Rabbit/Water and others

The Rabbit/Water knows how to listen. He is calm and reflective, and refrains from excess and dissipation. However, if he is to govern his life he must overcome a certain timidity and learn the art of indulging those passions he tends to recoil from, while at the same time controlling them. The Rabbit/Water has a horror of difficulties and hates to make a fuss. He will be a good craftsman and a prudent businessman. A pacifist and humanist, he will be more concerned with social problems and the battle against injustice than with spiritual matters.

He will be a good father, but not very stimulating. Mrs Rabbit/Water will be an attentive, tender-hearted mother, but will rarely make decisions.

Advice for a Rabbit/Water

You lack self-confidence. Leave your soft nest from time to time, forego your comfort and discard your slippers. You do not lack the ability to be dashing, but you always remain in the background. Be less passive; unless you want to perish from asphyxiation you must move about more. Do not continually rely on life-jackets; learn the crawl or build a raft.

A Rabbit/Water year

The culminating point of a Rabbit/Water year will be winter, a period of gestation.

A year of reflection rather than of action. However, do not become bogged down nor flounder about too much. If you do not sometimes leave your retreat you will have a false idea of things and of the world around you. Make this a year for projects and leave the flowers in your garden to bloom in their own good time. Practise cultivation in the fresh air, not in a greenhouse.

Historical example of a Rabbit/Water year 1951

In March, General MacArthur counter-attacked in Korea. He recaptured Seoul, the southern capital, and crossed the 38th parallel.

This war was the first to be fought under the idealistic banner of the United Nations and proved to be the last campaign they could support. The former pro-consul of Japan wished to carry the war into the mainland of China and there to assert by use of the nuclear weapon the beneficent powers he had exercised after the destruction of Hiroshima and Nagasaki. He argued that the initial aggression against Korea, although initiated by the Soviets, had been sustained by the Chinese alone who had gambled on the war being limited to the use of conventional weapons. Therefore America could equally gamble that Russia would not resort to their use in order to protect China.

These engaging equations were swiftly dismissed by President Truman. But MacArthur resisted. He resisted all attempts to negotiation, reasserted the need for a nuclear strike and sought thereby to reinstate Chiang-Kai-shek and to assert American dominance in China. Inflamed with the self-esteem he had garnered in Japan, MacArthur failed to appreciate that the vast territories of China were impervious to nuclear destruction and that their occupation under an American aegis would necessarily bring about a potent reaction from the Russians. Truman's policy accorded with the expressed view of the United Nations — to secure the independence of South Korea and otherwise to restore the status quo. Recalled to the Pentagon, MacArthur was greeted by the American people as a hero; but Truman neutralized him. Truman was a statesman. He was prepared to demonstrate that the United States would act to curb aggression; he himself would curb any instincts for wider conquests.

RABBIT/WOOD
(you were born in 1903 or 1963)

To the East, the wind blew in the sky and from its warm caress of the Earth, Wood was born.

Characteristics of the Rabbit/Wood
Wood is of the morning and of springtime. Its temperate nature loves harmony, beauty and elegance. It is an Element which suits the Rabbit perfectly. He will rediscover the mildness of the fertile and creative mid-season, which will restore his equilibrium, release his inventive powers and reinforce his taste for the beautiful. He will be pushed out of

his nest and discover the spectacle of dawn. This Element will develop in the Rabbit a sense of adventure, a passion for travel and a love of nature. But Wood is also a symbol of violence, even of destruction and self-destruction. Although he will not lose his dignity nor his reserve, the Rabbit/Wood will be vulnerable to internal jolts and passionate love storms which will leave him giddy and bewildered. If your instinctive impulses are allowed to dominate you, they will blind you. Overcome your aggressiveness; do not allow yourself to be drowned by your emotions.

Health of the Rabbit/Wood
The organ of Wood is the liver; its flavour is acid. The Rabbit/Wood will often be anxious, anguished and tormented. He will tend to worry and fret. Do not bite your paws, and be careful not to overeat.

The Rabbit/Wood and others
Socially, the Rabbit/Wood is relaxed and calm and well in control of his anguished nature which, if unrestrained, would lead him to fail in all his enterprises and be catastrophic for those around him. His tendency to be self-destructive would be nourished and lead him to ruin. Faced with established rules, the Rabbit/Wood opts for a supple attitude. He prefers to improvise and allow his imagination free rein, which encourages his creative spirit. The Rabbit/Wood has poetic gifts and is attracted to the arts in general — unless he chooses horticulture or landscaping, which can please his sense of beauty and harmony while fulfilling his need for space and liberty.

Advice for a Rabbit/Wood
You possess a good figure and are elegant, poetic and have an artistic soul. You do not appreciate restraints and obligations, so take responsibility for yourself and do not impose rigid restrictions on yourself or you will explode. Leave your anxiety in the cloakroom, polish your act as the

aesthetic seducer and allow yourself to enjoy the applause.

A Rabbit/Wood year

The culminating point of a Rabbit/Wood year will be spring, a period of growth and prosperity. He will be alive with a new energy urging him to create, whose principal source of inspiration will be nature. It is a year of harmony and suppleness which he must make use of with art and mastery. In some cases, however, the tendency may be reversed: there are criminal acts and conspiracies in the air.

Historical example of a Rabbit/Wood year 1963

John F. Kennedy's father was remembered in England with anger and resentment. He had not only scoffed at the government but at the country to which he was accredited as ambassador during the years of Hitler's rise to power and the war which followed. He appeared to represent the bleak lack of comprehension of the monied Puritan from the United States, embodying an ignorant contempt for the past and stultifying envy for those who claimed one.

Yet his son, when elected President of the United States, was greeted and acclaimed in England as elsewhere. In the early days of an optimistic decade, he came like a dawn, a new hope for the spirit of integrity and decency in the civilized world. His mistakes were quickly forgiven; his successes as quickly acclaimed. He revived the belief in the power and efficacy of American optimism, its innocence and its urgency, and he appeared to unite an understanding of the nature of the human predicament with a capacity to solve its immediate problems.

Yet Kennedy was probably better regarded anywhere than in his own country. His policies were resented and many of his measures obstructed in Congress. In Texas, he was warned, trouble might be expected when he visited Houston. His policies were not favoured there. To some extent, Houston represented the heartland of the right, bent to the very attitudes which Kennedy had publicly deplored.

Kennedy's assassination both shocked and alarmed the world. The Europeans in particular feared the discovery of some Soviet complicity. This was a foolish misjudgement. Khrushchev and Kennedy understood each other: neither wished the other to be replaced. It was to the credit of both the governments of the United States and of the Soviet Union that this dangerous theme was never allowed to develop. It has been said that Kennedy could never have fulfilled his programmes or his promise. His death marked an end to a potent inspiration to which even de Gaulle seemed willing to respond.

RABBIT/FIRE
(you were born in 1927)

Heat was born in the southern sky, descended to Earth and fertilized it. From their union, Fire was born.

Characteristics of the Rabbit/Fire

The Fire Element is of the midday, the South and summer. Fire is Yang; it is the Element which animates, quickens and transforms.

Fire, in a Rabbit with a Yin tendency, of the full moon in mid-autumn, will make him dynamic. This Element will catalyze your energy, releasing a boldness and rashness which will dominate your instinct for prudence and reserve. It will be an inner flame that strengthens your courage; a creative flame, a keen and rapid force and a giver of light. But it will also be a power which devours and consumes. The Rabbit should learn to control it, lest it become destructive; and maintain it, lest it goes out.

Health of the Rabbit/Fire

The organ of Fire is the heart; its flavour is bitter. Fire of summer and of the South, it will consume the Yin of the Rabbit. Be careful of changes in temperature. Avoid outbursts of anger and distrust your tendency towards aggressiveness — do not allow yourself to become violent. Keep a close watch on your heart. Eat vegetables rather than meat.

The Rabbit/Fire and others
Fire is often a symbol of war, passion and violence. The Rabbit/Fire prefers aggressiveness and open confrontation to diplomatic compromise; coming to terms is not his strong point. A man of action and combat, he combines energy with daring. However, due to his prudence and reserve, he will not hesitate, if need be, to send others to the frontline so that he can be the first to reap any rewards. The Rabbit/Fire will be artistic, original and anticonformist, and will be happy in this environment provided his life is well-organized.

Advice for a Rabbit/Fire
Although you are strongly attracted to distinguished and bold actions and wild adventures, you should remain faithful to your deepest nature. Reason should always be in control of your excesses, which are not always sincere unless they are symptomatic of an inner crisis and are thus therapeutic.

A Rabbit/Fire year
The culminating point of a Rabbit/Fire year will be summer, a period of creation, material and spiritual uplift and action, but often slightly consuming. The Rabbit will leave the full moon of mid-autumn to warm himself in the summer sun of the South. His Yin tendency will move towards the Great Yang, which will provide him with remarkable dynamism.

Historical example of a Rabbit/Fire year 1867
This was the year of the second Reform Bill in England

enacted by the Conservative government of Derby and Disraeli. Lord Derby later described it as 'a leap in the dark', for it was a measure which Gladstone and the Liberal party might more naturally have put in hand. The cynics regarded it as a measure to 'dish the Whigs' but Disraeli claimed that the policy it enshrined demonstrated that Conservative policy was the policy of true progress. Disraeli's biographer, Robert Blake, writes:* '. . . the picture of what happened has often been distorted. The most popular version . . . is that Disraeli enfranchised the householder at Gladstone's behest, in order to keep office; that the working-class household having received the vote from Disraeli said "thankyou Mr. Gladstone"; and accordingly voted him into power in 1868. His [Gladstone's] amendments were invariably defeated, and he fades into the background during the later stages of the debate. As for the gratitude of the working-class householders [they] . . . did not get on the register in time for the 1868 election . . . but if the Liberal myth dissolves on examination, so, too, does a scarcely less widely held Conservative one . . . . All the evidence of his contemporary papers suggests that Disraeli saw the electorate in traditional terms of rural voters being Conservative, urban voters Liberal; and that he thought of politics as a matter of "management" and "influence" in the old-fashioned sense, not mass persuasion of a new class.' Yet, as Blake concedes, many of the newly enfranchised in the towns did, in fact, tend to vote Conservative. Imperialism and social reform attracted them, a fact intuitively understood by Disraeli. That was not a proper subject for his papers on the Bill, however, which had to be fought on more formal grounds. In those fields Disraeli was a politician of genius and a parliamentarian of unrivalled skill.

*Disraeli, Robert Blake, London, 1966.

RABBIT/EARTH
(you were born in 1915 or 1975)

Earth was born from the slowly falling Elements of the sky at its humid zenith.

Characteristics of the Rabbit/Earth

This is an afternoon Earth, the humid and hot Earth of summer. It is the symbol of the well-cushioned, soft nest, of comfort and abundance; an Earth of slow and profound transformations. It is a blessing for the Rabbit, a warm refuge for repose and solitude, inviting him to meditate and dream. Here he will be far from the aggressions of the outside world, safe from indiscreet looks, trials and tribulations. But care is needed: the Rabbit tends to be a bit of a stay-at-home, and the Earth Element is likely to aggravate this tendency, turning him into a lazy and sated animal.

Health of the Rabbit/Earth

The Earth's organ is the spleen; its flavour is sweet. A sensualist, complete with moustache and cushions, inclined to the good life, the Rabbit/Earth should leave his nest and indulge in sports for the sake of his mental health. If the Rabbit/Earth does not rouse himself he will become a short-winded, fat miser.

The Rabbit/Earth and others

This Rabbit will certainly have his paws on the ground. Materialistic and prudent, he will be a good financier, subtle banker or a shrewd businessman. He will be the kind of whom one says 'he made himself through sheer hard work'. And this is true: he is a hard worker who accumulates the fruits of his efforts and will amass money and speculate with it. He possesses a strong family sense and will often be a despotic parent, brooding over his offspring to the point of smothering them.

Advice for a Rabbit/Earth

Above all, do not become too wrapped up in yourself. Broaden your horizons, take a holiday, mingle with others or participate in group work. Do not confine yourself to a world of mortgages and inventories. You need outdoor activity. Interest yourself in something other than your nest and your clover. Find a hobby. A little passion in your life would help to loosen your overly rigid life style.

A Rabbit/Earth year

The culminating point of a Rabbit/Earth year is summer. It is favourable year in which the Rabbit will no longer have to hunt to feed himself and he will be served on a silver platter. Thus freed from daily obligations, the Rabbit should offer his services to some charitable activity. Be watchful of your attitude towards your personal comforts — you could well become narcissistic.

Historical example of a Rabbit/Earth year 1795

The occupation of Holland by the French, who renamed it the Batavian Republic, directed the attention of the English to the Dutch possessions in the East Indies. In a deep maritime thrust they captured Capetown and Ceylon before investing the former colonies of Holland. Another force was sent to contest the possession of the French West Indian islands, the very troops promised for an attack on the French Riviera designed to coincide with a new campaign by the Austrians. This dispersal of naval forces weakened the blockading fleet off Toulon from which the French fleet escaped intact to secure a great Levenat convoy bound for England. Thus although France was not secure she was no longer in imminent danger; the absolute stringencies imposed by Robespierre and the Terror were no longer acknowledged to be necessary for the public safety. In this young republic given to extremes the reaction was forthright. Robespierre and his chief supporters were arrested, tried and sent to the guillotine on 27 July.

The atmosphere in France changed to one of almost drunken levity. Those younger members of the nobility who had survived took the lead in promoting a reign of pleasure, affecting an extravagance and sophistication of manner as extreme as their dress. Their idol Mme Tallien, on the other hand, affected a minimum of clothing at her celebrated salons. The wealth and interests of the middle classes quickly resumed their sway and the new constitution promulgated in September was expressly designed to produce a weak executive answerable to the propertied class. This development was resented by the royalists of the extreme right and the ultras of the left. Their insurrection proved a turning point in the history of France, for Barras called on the young Napoleon Bonaparte to restore order. It was thus that he came to command the armies with which he would conquer Italy.

RABBIT/METAL
(you were born in 1939)

In the sky, coming from the West, drought grazed the skin of the Earth and gave birth to Metal. Winds come from the far-away steppes seeking the vital sap.

Characteristics of the Rabbit/Metal
Metal is of the night, of autumn and cold. It symbolizes clarity, purity and precision. Its tendency is to be cutting, rigid and chaste, its comments harsh. The Rabbit/Metal will

oscillate between beauty and destruction. He will be expert at putting his plans into effect. At harvest-time, he will be the blade that gleans. Alas, too rigorous a regime will bring sadness and moroseness.

It can be a beneficial time for the Rabbit who is often unselfconscious, detached and prudent, bringing him a sense of responsibility and an indication of the plan he should follow. Unfortunately, rigid plans do not suit his supple spine. Therefore the Rabbit should beware of excess and recognize that strength of purpose does not necessarily mean stiffness. Moreover, the Metal Element is attracted to mystical perspectives which, although not a summons to an authentic vocation, can become an alibi or a dangerous refuge for him. The Rabbit/Metal seeks solitude, but sometimes has difficulty attaining harmony between his body and his soul.

Health of the Rabbit/Metal
Metal's organ is the lung; its flavour is pungent. In seeking an equilibrium, the Rabbit/Metal must keep a watch on his lungs, for their proper function is a source of physical and spiritual harmony. Blockages of all kinds can be dangerous. Do not allow your organs and heart to dry up!

The Rabbit/Metal and others
The Rabbit/Metal is energetic, constant and a man of his word. He can be a warrior or a man of the law. He commands, judges and decides. He has a good feel for organization, but at times may be slightly too blunt in his approach — plain-speaking will come more easily to him than tact and diplomacy. Maintain the moral and physical suppleness of the Rabbit; a stiff neck and a dry, cold heart are not in the nature of your symbolic animal. Rediscover agility, grace and patience. Be energetic, but do not forget that the excessive, in any form, turns against its author. File down your claws and become more supple; indulgence is not necessarily self-indulgence.

Advice for a Rabbit/Metal

Do some relaxing exercises or yoga. Write poems and listen to music; do not encase yourself in an iron corset — it will harm your fur.

A Rabbit/Metal year

The culminating point of a Rabbit/Metal year will be autumn. You will often experience a loss of energy and dynamism, and suffer from depression and a lack of self-confidence. This may perhaps be due to a lack of suppleness or a certain moral stiffness which does not suit your deepest nature. A period of waiting and uncertainty.

Historical example of a Rabbit/Metal year 1519

The Emperor Maximilian I was dead. His eldest grandson, Charles King of Spain and the Two Sicilies, ruler of Burgundy and the Netherlands was the natural claimant by blood. Francis I claimed the historic right as King of France and heir to Charlemagne. Charles put himself forward as a true German and the only person with sufficient resources to resist the Turks, then threatening the entire fabric of Christian Europe. Francis replied that the Empire was not the monopoly of one family, that he alone as the true and historic heir to Charlemagne embodied the chivalry of the civilized world and was the natural guardian of its values against the rapacity of the Spanish King.

However, it was not these formal appeals and dissertations which were to secure the election of the Emperor. The decisive advantage lay with Charles who had immediate access to the resources of the great Fugger banking house in Antwerp. No one could then match them in experience or influence. It was they who secured Charles's election; but not without conditions. The so-called 'Capitulation of Election' bound Charles to observe all princely privileges and to obtain the approval of the

Electors to legislation, treaties, taxes and imperial policy. The hiring of foreign mercenaries was forbidden him.

These were conditions which Francis would have found intolerable but they were acceptable to Charles. At heart he was an ascetic, indeed he was to end his days in monastic seclusion. He wished only to guide imperial policy towards that unity of Christendom laboured for by the medieval papacy.

Analogical Table
of the Different Elements

Elements	Wood	Fire	Earth	Metal	Water
Years ending in	3 and 8	2 and 7	0 and 5	4 and 9	1 and 6
Colours	Green	Red	Yellow	White	Blue
Seasons	Spring	Summer	End of summer	Autumn	Winter
Climates	Wind	Heat	Humid	Dry	Cold
Flavours	Acid	Bitter	Sweet	Pungent	Salty
Principal organ	Liver	Heart	Spleen	Lungs	Kidneys
Secondary organ	Gallbladder	Small intestine	Stomach	Large intestine	Bladder
Food	Wheat, poultry	Rice, lamb	Corn, beef	Oats, horse	Peas, pork

Table of Harmony Between the Elements

		Wood Female	Fire Female	Earth Female	Metal Female	Water Female
○○○ Excellent prosperity	Male Wood	●●	○	○○○	○	○○
○○ Good harmony, understanding	Male Fire	○	○	○○	●	●●
○ Effort needed	Male Earth	●●	○○	○○	○○○	●
● Rivalries and problems of reciprocal domination	Male Metal	○	●●	●	●●	○○○
●● Misunderstanding and incomprehension	Male Water	○○	●●	●	○○○	○

THE
FOUR SEASONS
OF
THE RABBIT

四季

If you were born in spring

Rabbit/Aries

The positive points of this alliance result from the profound differences that exist between a Rabbit and an Aries. The Rabbit is sedentary, prudent and peaceful (do not forget that the sign of the Rabbit is also a Cat, and neither are especially daring). On the other hand, those born under the sign of Aries are impulsive, active and spontaneous. If all that is put into the same pot, boiled and stirred long enough, a harmonious mixture is produced. Thus we find a Rabbit/Aries who is reasonably moderate and active and who, with a shrewd eye, murmurs to us from his comfortable cushion, 'excess in anything is a defect'. Then, quicker than lightning, he snatches a pawful of clover, swallows it whole and licks his lips with an innocent air. In sum, an effective Rabbit who does well in his Rabbit profession.

There is obviously a lively combination of qualities in this mixture which may be usefully exploited in financial and professional areas: daring and prudence combine to avoid the ultraconservative as well as more risky schemes.

However, the Rabbit/Aries also has a slightly superficial quality, a need to shine in any field and to impose his views on matters which he does not really know much about. At the same time, he is sociable and friendly.

Rabbit/Taurus

The Rabbit/Taurus is either a delightful or maddening person, depending on whether or not one can adapt to the kind of life he likes to lead. He is firmly sedentary and attached to his slippers and garden.

For him, security is an end in itself and, to obtain it, he is capable of unusual effort, applying himself with perseverance and a remarkable sense of reality. He will be a prudent, clever, far-sighted businessman. If he does not climb to the top rung in international finance, it will be because at six in the evening something inside his head reminds him with the sound of sweet music that it is time to go home to dinner. He can work overtime in order to buy his son a bicycle, but never in order to hear himself called 'Chief'.

The Rabbit/Taurus is affectionate with his family and friends and likes nothing better than to gather them together at his own fireside. However, harmony is dramatically vulnerable to outside circumstances which might intrude upon him. The unforeseen is his nightmare, and he can be knocked completely off balance by an unexpected event affecting his security or wealth. A true Rabbit/Taurus will have a great deal of trouble not breaking a paw if he falls out of a window.

Rabbit/Gemini

This is the most agile and elusive of Rabbits, as difficult to capture as to hold. Always playing with danger, he never falls for the home-and-hearth life style so fatal for other Rabbits, but travels when he pleases, eats when he is hungry, allows himself to be caressed if he wishes and then disappears. He is very much a Rabbit who walks alone, wherever he feels inclined. There is nothing of the surburban commuter about this Rabbit.

This is not to suggest that the Rabbit/Gemini is not sociable. He likes conversation and to romp in gay company, but never to the extent of having to depend on others. He is as free within himself as he is independent of others. Structures and barriers are unknown to him; he follows only his fantasy and curiosity.

He is certainly unstable, yet remains extraordinarily adroit. He can get out of the most desperate of situations: when he is supposedly in prison for swindling, you will see his photo in the newspaper with the Prime Minister. Seeking surprises, he greatly enjoys causing them.

The Rabbit/Gemini is often unfaithful in love. He prefers variety to the daily routine in love affairs and friendship. Emotional rather than sensitive, it is not easy to move him to pity. Yet in his heart of hearts he fears solitude, and in this state is very vulnerable. It is up to others to know when to try and profit from this.

If you were born in summer
Rabbit/Cancer

These two signs share many tastes, in particular the apparent contradiction between their love of home-life and their taste for independence.

The Rabbit/Cancer draws in its claws, is affectionate and not particularly active. He is ready to make many compromises in order to preserve his security and to defend himself from the outside world. Faced with a problem, he pretends to sleep and develops a formidable case of inertia. But mistrust a sleeping Rabbit; pushed too far, he can become a ball of pins.

The Rabbit/Cancer likes to dream; sometimes he will do no more than daydream instead of setting about his tasks. Given enough encouragement, he will make an effort and complete what he has undertaken to do. He is somewhat erratic in this way. In his own world he likes to be paternalistic and often boasts a bit just to attract attention. Needing to feel in the centre of things, he badly needs to be taken care of. Moreover, everyone excuses his moments of boastfulness and touchiness, for he is amiable and faithful. He prefers the hearth to humid nights outdoors.

Rabbit/Leo

A royal Rabbit: his robe is sumptuous and he cares for it. He also tends to nurse his image and tries to live a life which is basically respectable. He enjoys his ease and tranquillity, but he quivers with pleasurable anticipation at the idea of competition: he immediately sees himself enthroned on a red satin cushion with an Order strung round his neck.

On the whole, he has an even and sociable disposition. He enjoys giving parties in his house, loves luxury and appreciates beauty and lovely objects. He also likes good food. His weak point is that he depends on a settled life. It is not that he lacks courage, but that he is by nature unwilling to face up to unforeseen mishaps or to anything which upsets his plans. He does not like to fail, detests promiscuity, vulgarity or even negotiating a mud-puddle. If totally put out he will at first panic and then, provided he can see his way clearly and is satisfied that the trouble is worth his attention, he will attack. This Rabbit is not bred for navigating in troubled waters; moreover, he hates water.

Rabbit/Virgo

Do not expect this prudent and discreet Rabbit to come up to a stranger and rub against his legs. Distrustful and distant, he advances slowly and methodically, ever on the alert. The Rabbit/Virgo will never willingly expose himself to danger.

He is an attentive and virtuous person, a stickler for honour, justice and duty. He can be annoying because at times he can be tiresomely wordy. He is so afraid of being caught making a mistake — and having to pay dearly for it — that he carefully calculates his approach. 'Once bitten twice shy' fits him like a glove. In fact, one often has the impression that his tenacious memory of past difficulties surfaces whenever he must grapple with a serious problem.

Foreseeing and wise, the Rabbit/Virgo succeeds without creating an uproar and knows how to gain the approval of his fellows, whose liberty he respects. However, in later years he can become dogmatic and grouchy, fuming for hours because his nest has been disorganized or his clover badly prepared.

If you were born in autumn
Rabbit/Libra

Do you remember the Cheshire Cat in 'Alice in Wonderland'? Seated in a tree, he would make himself visible and then disappear; only his smile would remain. There is something of this attitude in the Rabbit/Libra. He dislikes extremes and tense situations. He quietly nibbles his grass, moving slowly, an inch at a time, concerned with preserving the harmony of the moment and its particular ambience. He seeks refinement and certain aesthetic values.

A wordly and sociable Rabbit, he selects those in whom he has noted moral and physical elegance. He behaves with infinite charm, with bows and gracious gestures, preoccupied with a profound desire to please. He is capable of making many concessions to avoid a dispute but he detests being cornered and forced to make a hasty decision. It is then that he will resemble Alice's cat, climbing into his tree and observing you at length, with a debonair and sneering air. You will be the first to give up.

If he is in trouble, he is much more adaptable than the other Rabbits; he always lands on his feet and succeeds tactfully and without haste. Potentially a good diplomat, brilliant lawyer or talented artist, he is not made for manual activities, such as sawing wood.

Rabbit/Scorpio

He is soft, undulating and slightly fiendish. Sociable in appearance, he makes marvellous use of his charm and amiability curling up on your lap. To persuade you of his innocence he would be prepared to play with a doll and rattle.

But as soon as he opens his mouth he becomes scratchy, which comes as a surprise. In fact, the Rabbit/Scorpio is either an accomplished egotist, a refined opportunist, or a chronic neurotic who is anxious and ill-at-ease. He tricks his friends and shamelessly profits from them. The notion of good and evil, dear to our civilization, is simply an inconvenience to him. He would like to be tranquil, which he attains by sitting in the sun. But then night comes and, in spite of himself, he becomes transformed into a magician and a sorcerer. Perhaps the Rabbit/Scorpio remembers, deep in his subconscious, when he was once thrown onto sacrificial pyres, which is why he is uneasy.

His charm is fascinating, his power of conviction astonishing. He likes nothing better than to surprise his associates, alternating softness with sudden aggression. He is extremely prudent, perspicacious and intuitive: do not attempt to deceive him or try to make him believe that the moon is made of green cheese. He will throw himself at you and deliver a beautifully executed right hook.

In love he is sincere, but has trouble putting himself in another's place.

Rabbit/Sagittarius

At first glance this is a truly marvellous Rabbit. He is sociable and well-balanced; his daily routine does not obsess him. He is perhaps the only Rabbit capable of blossoming in his role as domestic as well as wild animal; he has both elements within him and passes from one to the other with marvellous ease. He is easy to live with and always in good humour.

But he is emotional rather than truly sensitive, very ambitious and sometimes egocentric; his generosity is only bestowed on those who are lucky enough to share his point of view. He likes to attract attention — to convince, persuade, seduce and shine. As soon as he sees a podium he wants to make a speech or, if he is timid, dreams of doing so.

An adventurous and audacious Rabbit, he is also a conformist who is strongly attached to his personal principles of honour, independence, and so on. He can be annoying due to his dogmatic side, and seductive due to his spontaneous and warm side. The Rabbit/Sagittarius has many defects, but he will never stab you in the back.

If you were born in winter
Rabbit/Capricorn

If you are feeling lonely one day and go to the pet shop to seek a companion, you will easily recognize a Rabbit/Capricorn; he remains apart from the others and will not come to charm you by rubbing against the bars of the cage. On the contrary, he will be seated at the far end, looking vaguely scornful. If you try to caress him he may even spit, so that you understand that not just anybody is allowed to paw him. But if you take him home and treat him with respect and pay him exclusive attention, you will have won a prize. For the Rabbit/Capricorn is the most faithful and stable of Rabbits. He is neither caressing nor demonstrative, but defends his home better than a watchdog; he can be counted on in all circumstances. He will not adapt in the face of catastrophe, for that is not his strong point, but he will cling heroically.

He is effective and persevering in his material life. Many lost Rabbits will travel over long distances, braving a thousand dangers to find their way home; they must be Capricorns born in a year of the Rabbit.

Rabbit/Aquarius

This combination will diminish considerably the egotistic side of the Rabbit because they are interested in the world surrounding their personal universe. The Rabbit/Aquarius rarely remains a traveller, a vagabond, keeping up friendly relations with almost everyone and enjoying a fair-haired Rabbit in each port. More gifted for friendship than love, he will be spontaneously unselfish. However, he is often a bit absent-minded and distracted.

Extremely creative and completely anticonformist, the Rabbit/Aquarius does not spend much time on reflection but his intellectual activity far exceeds his physical activity. He does not depend on guide lines, and a conventional scale of values will only imprison him. He navigates by guesswork, free as the air and as supple and whimsical as curling breezes. A precious and devoted friend, he knows nothing of jealousy but he is an unstable lover. However, he is marvellously tolerant, even slightly devil-may-care, and does not ask of others more than he does of himself, so one can willingly pardon him.

Rabbit/Pisces

The Rabbit/Pisces often lacks the most elementary practical

sense. Plunged into the most coolly delicious stream, he will dream of having a paraffin heater to increase the temperature. He is never competely content; he always needs a little bit more.

The Rabbit/Pisces is an accomplished dreamer who, if really motivated, can become a formidable opportunist. But this does not happen every day. The rest of the time he is half asleep, imagining terrible dramas, which tires him out. He is neither very persevering nor very active, but he is adorable and affectionate. He also needs a daily ration of affection and tenderness. Give him a tape recording which says 'I love you' every three minutes and do not be stingy with showing him your feelings. Your Rabbit/Pisces will then be in his element.

THE
I CHING

易经

THE I CHING AND THE RABBIT

In the I Ching game, you ask a question and you obtain an answer. It is therefore a divining game. But the question you ask is posed through your Rabbit identity; the wheels, the complex mechanism of your mind and spirit, begin to turn. You ask a Rabbit question and the I Ching answers with a Rabbit 'solution', on which you then meditate as a Rabbit before arriving at a Rabbit conclusion.

The player is presented with a hexagram which contains the 'hypothesis-response' to his question, or, more exactly, a synthesis of forces affecting the concern or event inquired about.

For you, Master Rabbit, here are the sixty-four hexagrams of the I Ching and sixty-four Rabbit hypotheses.

How to proceed
1. The question
Ask a question regarding any problem at all, past, present or future, personally concerning you. (If the question concerns a friend, consult the I Ching game in the book corresponding to his Chinese sign.)

2. Method of play
It must be done with concentration.
Take **three ordinary and similar coins** — for example, three 50p coins.
Heads will equal the number 3.
Tails will equal the number 2.
Throw the coins.
If the result is two coins showing Heads and one Tails, write 3 + 3 + 2. You thus obtain a total of 8 which you represent by a continuous line: ———

Draw the same continuous line if you have three coins showing Heads (3 + 3 + 3 = 9).

If you throw two coins showing Tails and one Heads (2 + 2 + 3 = 7), or all three showing Tails (2 + 2 + 2 = 6), draw two separate lines: ▬ ▬

To sum up, 8 and 9 correspond to: ▬▬▬ (Yin)
6 and 7 correspond to: ▬ ▬ (Yang)

Repeat this operation *six times*, noting at the time of each throw the figure obtained on a piece of paper, proceeding from the first to the sixth figure, from bottom to top.

The final result, including a trigram from the bottom, or lower trigram (example: ▤), and a trigram of the top, or upper trigram (example: ▤), will be a hexagram of the I Ching. In our example this would look like:

Now merely look for the hexagram number in the table on page 78 , and then consult the list of hexagrams with their descriptions to find the given answer. *In our example*, the hexagram obtained is number 63, entitled **After completion**.

Table of Hexagrams

Trigrams	Upper lines ☰	☷	☳
Lower lines			
☰	1	11	34
☷	12	2	16
☳	25	24	51
☵	6	7	40
☶	33	15	62
☴	44	46	32
☲	13	36	55
☱	10	19	54

Use this table to find the number of your hexagrams. The meeting point between the lower and upper trigrams indicates the number of the hexagram that you are seeking.

☵	☶	☴	☳	☱
5	26	9	14	43
8	23	20	35	45
3	27	42	21	17
29	4	59	64	47
39	52	53	56	31
48	18	57	50	28
63	22	37	30	49
60	41	61	38	58

THE HEXAGRAMS OF THE RABBIT

CH'IEN

1 *The creative:* Energy, strength and will, the creative spirit. Master Rabbit will be in his element, he who knows so well how to combine prudence and reserve with a fertile imagination, sometimes reaching beyond the knowable to where dreams and reality are blended.

K'UN

2 *The receptive:* You are bound to the Earth Mother. It will not be difficult for you to become aware of the elements surrounding you, for they are your tools: even when astride two worlds, do not forget them.

CHUN

3 *The initial difficulty:* Unravel, clear away, seek the cause of the trouble. The situation is delicate and there are many obstacles, but a bit of perseverance will enable you to succeed.

MÊNG

4 *Youthful folly:* 'It is not I who seeks the young fool, but the young fool who seeks me.' Generously support those who ask your advice, but do not allow yourself to be trapped.

HSÜ

5 *Waiting:* It is unnecessary to draw you a picture; waiting too is an art — and difficult to master.

SUNG

6 *Conflict:* Disguise and diplomacy are better than open warfare. The Rabbit who dislikes becoming involved or being in the forefront will opt for this technique.

SHIH

7 *The army:* Submission and discipline for a collective aim. Know how to join in: although you practise war on your own, with strategies and attacks which have ripened for a long time, know how to bend to the common rule.

PI

8 *Holding together (union):* Strength lies in union. A large bone for the Rabbit to swallow, a defender of 'everyone for himself'.

SHIAO CH'U

9 *The taming power of the small:* This is not the moment to use force, for you do not have enough strength. Goodness and gentleness will give better results.

LÜ

10 *Treading:* 'Tread on the tail of the Tiger, he does not bite man.' Pull in your claws, relax and place your paws between the stripes on the Tiger; it is not difficult, a simple question of balance.

T'AI

11 *Peace:* Or the harmony of opposites, which is always delicate to achieve. When dialogue is not possible, confusion reigns; choose peace, but remain vigilant.

THE RABBIT

P'I

12 *Standstill:* It is better to know how to pull back than to attack when the hour is not right. The art of waiting is a form of action; nothing good can come from hasty acts.

T'UNG JÊN

13 *Fellowship with men:* Even spiritual work is more difficult to accomplish with men than without. But there is work that one cannot accomplish alone. So, forget your egotistical preoccupations and spontaneously help those whose aims are worthy of your esteem.

TA YU

14 *Possession in great measure:* Whether this be material or spiritual, if you neglect it and fail to bring it to fruition good opportunities are likely to be missed.

CH'IEN

15 ▦ *Modesty:* Ride out the storm, trim your sails and seek the horizontal; water is its symbol. Exaggeraton in any field will incur disappointments.

YÜ

16 ▦ *Enthusiasm:* Although restraint and hesitation are valuable, it is time to take risks; do not play hide-and-seek with reality. You have imagination — use it.

SUI

17 *Following:* After seduction and the use of an 'iron fist in a velvet glove', you now have only to convince with a dose of powerful speech-making.

KU

18 *Work on what has been spoiled:* One does not cure the bad with indifference, nor difficulties with abandon. It is not advisable to make your nest in a minefield unless you know how to defuse the mines.

LIN

19 *Approach:* Do not forget that what you call 'today' is already the past. Rather, be preoccupied with the near future. Try to evolve and progress; you will meet with success.

KUAN

20 *Contemplation:* A Rabbit at the summit of a tower will be visible from afar. Your virtue will be put to a difficult test, for in making it public, you expose yourself to the danger of setting yourself up as an example.

SHIH HO

21 *Biting through (or clearly defined penalties):* Lying is not profitable; in giving it shape, think of the consequences. No liaison or association is reliable because the foundations are rotten. The house will fall down. So, burn the bad roots and attack, if only to set an example.

PI

22 *Grace:* Even when planning a sauce for the fish, there will always be bones to swallow.

PO

23 *Splitting apart:* Be on your guard, the edifice threatens to collapse from within. Be careful of what pours down.

FU

24 *Return (the turning point):* After spending some time with your head under a cushion, you can come up for air; the danger is past, the wheel turns.

WU WANG

25 *Innocence:* 'Man has received from heaven an essentially good nature to direct him in all his acts.' Your instinct does not mislead you; but it should guide rather than direct you.

TA CH'U

26 *The taming of the great:* Power and strength. This depends on your capacity for renewal. Do not fall asleep on your laurels.

I

27 The corners of the mouth: Symbol of nourishment of the body and the spirit: tell me what you eat and read and I will tell you who you are. There is no need to become a vegetarian in order to read the great philosophers. Be authentic.

TA KUO

28 *Preponderance of the great:* It is silly to try and move the mountain when one can go round it.

K'AN

29 *Fathomless water:* The danger comes from outside. Remain calm; pay no attention to fear and master your panic.

LI

30 *Clinging, fire:* Do not concentrate all your energies on a spider when the dogs are barking at the door. The danger is there, so do not weave your own cord but learn to unknot it.

HSIEN

31 *Influence:* You have charm and others are sensitive to it; you have fine qualities and they are noticed. Do not be capricious; drop your mask and take risks. Otherwise you will miss an opportunity — perhaps the opportunity of your lifetime.

HÊNG

32 *Duration:* To avoid stagnating, question yourself; this is painful but effective. Understand that when the wine has been uncorked, it has to be drunk.

TUN

33 *Retreat:* Without constraint or despair, therefore it can even lead to a tactical victory. Do not think of it as a rout.

TA CHUANG

34 *The power of the great:* Might allied with movement becomes a powerful attraction. There is danger of burning one's wings, like the moth and the flame.

CHIN

35 *Progress:* He who possesses radiance does not feel the need to shine. Do not refuse the earthenware bowl and demand a silver bowl; both contain food.

MING I

36 *Darkening of the light:* Do the housework, provide yourself with candles and wait for the storm to pass to relight the flame.

CHIA JÊN

37 *The family:* Has a good deal to be said for it, especially for a Rabbit who loves his tranquillity and comfort. If it seems like a prison, he should not forget that it is he who holds the key.

K'UEI

38 *Opposition:* Does not exist unless one creates it. Respect the harmony of opposites. Do not be opposed to the world.

CHIEN

39 *Obstruction:* Is not equivocal; jump the obstacle, undermine it or go round it. Refuse neither a rope, ladder, nor a helping hand.

HSIEH

40 *Deliverance:* It is today that you must set to work for tomorrow. Do not encumber yourself with painful memories; think of future trials; work to reestablish order.

SUN

41 *Decrease:* Hard to imagine for a fashionable man-about-town, a lover of luxury and ostentation. Flee from pomp, put out the chandeliers and light the candles. They are more poetic and economic.

I

42 *Increase:* Make the most of each minute, involve yourself and be opportunistic; even if you are anxious, keep smiling.

KUAI

43 *Breakthrough:* You cannot make an omelette without breaking eggs; the truth is not always good to hear, but it has to be said.

KOU

44 *Coming to meet:* Do not forget that certain concessions, even if they are humiliating, can reestablish equilibrium — but know how to choose your partner.

TS'UI

45 *Gathering together:* Around a family or a community. However, there is danger of infiltration; distrust unknown elements.

SHÊNG

46 *Pushing upwards:* The Rabbit should prove that he is meticulous and neglects nothing. He will mount the great staircase step by step or, if he feels too tired, will take the lift.

K'UN

47 *Oppression:* Your handsome speeches are no longer effective; they put your audience to sleep; you are losing punch. Do not wait to be backed into a corner before reacting; take a tonic and learn to jump on to the perch.

CHING

48 *The well:* Act on yourself, on nature and things without, however, changing vital structures.

KO

49 *Revolution:* Should not be carried out in the privacy of one's room. Do not fear eventual confrontations, for they will be positive; anticipate them if you do not want them to fall on your head.

TING

50 *The cauldron:* Symbol of the five Elements — Earth, Wood, Fire, Water and Metal. Work to nourish yourself physically and materially. Bread and knowledge do not fall from the sky.

CHÊN

51 *The arousing (shock, thunder):* Will be capable of awakening you and making you aware. Do not, however, change your itinerary; keep calm and accept the trials, for they are a part of your voyage.

KÊN

52 *Keeping still:* Let the tempest pass; find calm within yourself before confronting the tumult outside.

CHIEN

53 *Development (gradual progress):* Accept that you must sometimes bow; it is good for the health and makes one appreciate the vertical position.

KUEI MEI

54 *The bride:* Even if one plays at heartaches, get hold of yourself before succumbing.

FÊNG

55 *Abundance:* Will do no harm, but do not sink into complacence, the mother of egotism. For a time glide in its arms, but be careful of the fall.

LÜ

56 *The wanderer:* Since no one is a prophet in his own country, exercise your talents elsewhere. One must know how to detach oneself, to leave before sinking. Do not grumble — swim!

SUN

57 *The gentle:* The wind blows without violence, but penetrates where it wishes. Do likewise.

TUI

58 *The serene, the joyous:* Learn how to share and communicate. Persevere, but with suppleness.

HUAN

59 *Dissolution:* Be careful of egotism. By turning round and round on yourself, you will end by biting your tail.

CHIEH

60 *Limitation:* Should be understood as a means, not an end. It is not by crawling on your knees that you will be pardoned.

CHUNG FU

61 *Inner truth:* The way is not necessarily the Way. Do not seek to communicate what is incommunicable. Those who enclose God in words may become all-powerful, but only in the realm of words.

HSIAO KUO

62 *Preponderance of the small:* Even the most beautiful sand castles are carried away by the sea. It is folly to build great projects when one possesses only small means.

CHI CHI

63 *After completion:* The prince can become a merchant, but the merchant will never become a prince.

WEI CHI

64 *Before completion:* The seaweed clings to the rock in order to survive, not in the hope of becoming a rock; but joining the rock it welcomes the wave.